Once upon a time, there was a girl named Joy,

With skin as black as coal,
so strong and oh so proud.

She studied in a School,
             where everyone was fair,

And she stood out,
             with her skin so dark and rare.

Joy loved to play,
          and dance in the rain,

And sing with the birds,
          with joy and no restrain.

But the other girls,
      they often teased and would say,

"Why not be like us,
      with skin that's light and gay?"

But Joy, she just smiled

and

would answer each day

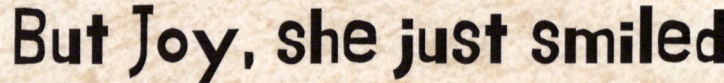

"I'm black all year, and that's okay!"

And soon enough,
      the other girls began to see,

That Joy's black skin was unique
          and so very pretty.

They would play together,
         and laugh with delight,

And learned to appreciate,
      each other's differences with sight.

Joy realized, that black skin was more than just a hue,

It represented strength, resilience and culture that was true.

And she embraced it,
 with pride and joy, every day,

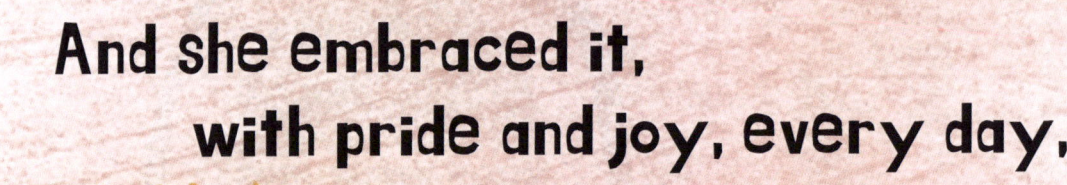

Showing the world, the beauty of black skin in every possible way.

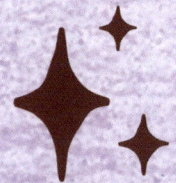

So remember, it doesn't matter
               what they say,
Being yourself is the best,
               in every single way.
  And just like Joy,
               you can shine bright,
Just be who you are,
               with all of your might.

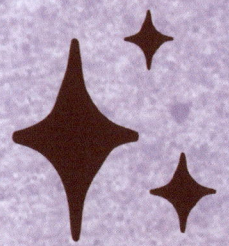

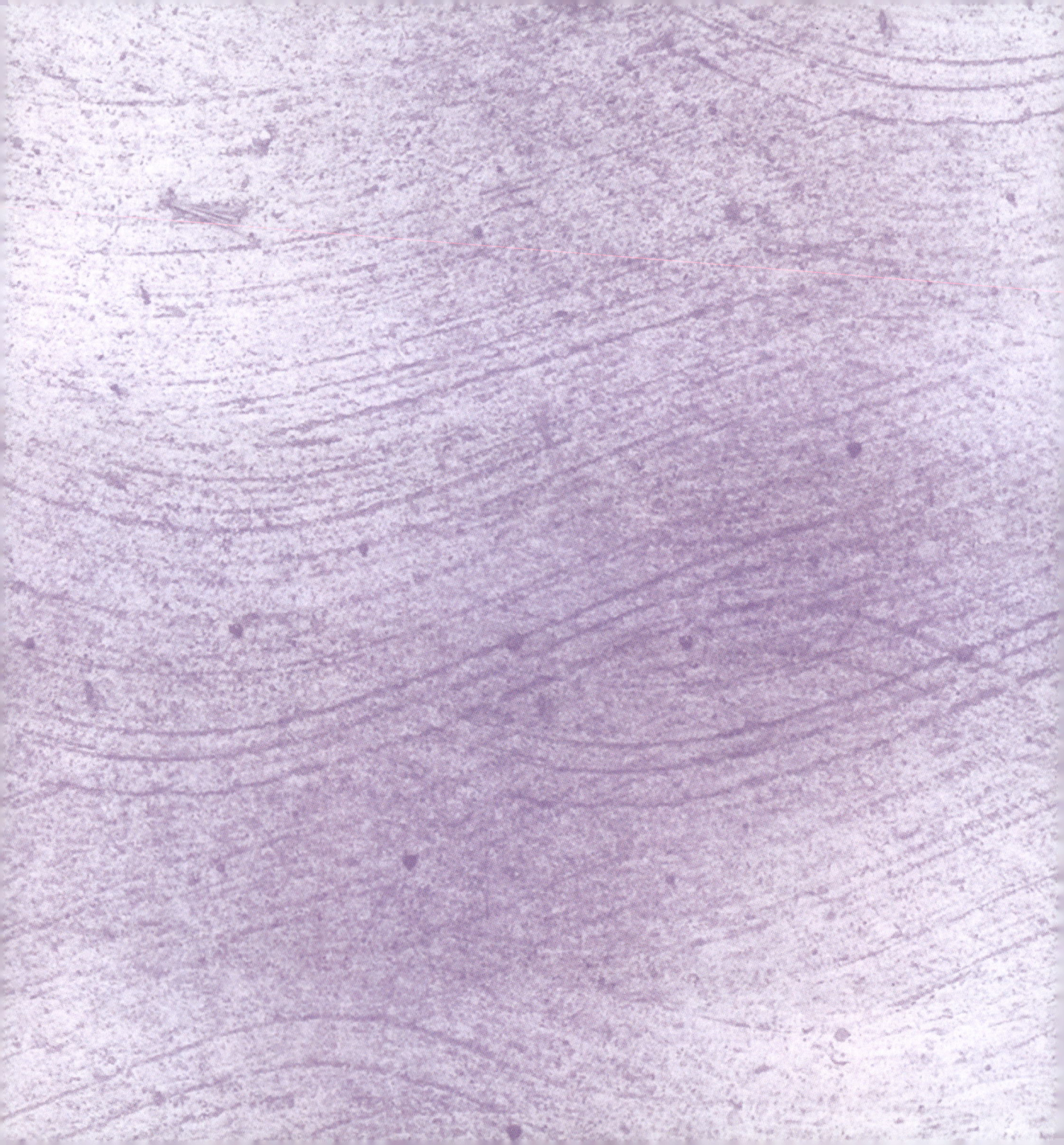

Printed in Great Britain
by Amazon